Katie Meets the Impressionists

James Mayhew

ORCHARD BOOKS

For my sister, the original 'Katie'

J.M

For more about Impressionist painters turn to the end of the book.

ORCHARD BOOKS
96 Leonard Street, London EC2A 4XD
Orchard Books Australia
32/45-51 Huntley Street, Alexandria, NSW 2015
ISBN 1 86039 018 8 (hardback)
ISBN 1 86039 768 9 (paperback)
First published in Great Britain in 1997
First paperback publication in 1998
Text and illustrations © James Mayhew 1997
The right of James Mayhew to be identified as the author and illustrator
of this work has been asserted by him in accordance with the
Copyright, Designs and Patents Act, 1988.
A CIP catalogue record for this book is available
from the British Library.
Printed in Belgium

11 13 15 17 19 20 18 16 14 12

It was Grandma's birthday and for a special treat she had taken Katie to the art gallery. Katie loved the gallery because you never knew what you were going to see there.

"Look at the flowers in the paintings," said Grandma.

"I can only see blobs," said Katie.

"The pictures are made up of blobs," said Grandma.

"But when you stand well back the blobs make a picture."

Katie wandered off into the next room to try. There she saw a painting called *The Luncheon* by Claude Monet and when she stood back, Katie could see a garden.

'Grandma would love flowers like those for her birthday,' she thought. She closed her eyes and sniffed. She was sure she could smell the flowers.

And when Katie opened her eyes, there she was, amongst the daisies, hollyhocks, roses and sunflowers.

"Can I pick some flowers?" said Katie to the little boy, who was called Jean.

Jean called his mother and nanny over and spoke to them in French.

"*Un bouquet?*" said his mother. "*Oui*, Jean, you go and help the girl."

So Jean and Katie gathered flowers together.

"Are you going to paint them?" he asked.

"No, they are for my Grandma," said Katie.

"Papa paints flowers," said Jean. "I'll show you."

Jean took Katie to a room full of pictures, like a small gallery.
"This is Papa's studio," he said. "He's a famous painter
called Claude Monet."

"I'm good at painting," said Katie."Let's have a go?"

They mixed the paint on palettes with brushes and found canvases to paint on.

They painted portraits of each other using blobs, just like real painters.

"Now I'd better get back to Grandma," said Katie and they went out into the garden.

"Will you come another day?" asked Jean.

"I'll try," said Katie. She picked up the bunch of flowers and, waving goodbye, climbed through the frame into the gallery.

Katie saw that the bunch of flowers was beginning to wilt. "What I need is some water," she said, looking around the gallery.

She saw a painting called *A Girl With a Watering Can*, by Pierre-Auguste Renoir. Katie looked around her to make sure no one was watching her, and climbed inside.

"Can I have some water for my flowers?" said Katie.
The little girl put the flowers into her watering can.
"*Voila!*" she said. But the flowers still drooped and
flopped over.

"Come and pick some more!" said the girl.
So Katie and the girl trampled through
the garden picking flowers. Katie pretended
it was a jungle and that she was a panther
chasing the girl.

Suddenly there was a terrible scream. It was the girl's
mother. "You have ruined my garden!" she shouted.

"It wasn't me," said the girl. "It was her," and she
pointed at Katie.

"Come here you naughty child," said the mother.

But Katie ran for the picture frame and leapt into
the gallery, leaving the flowers scattered behind her.

Katie sighed. She didn't dare go back to fetch the
flowers. She went to look at the other pictures.
There were a lot of pictures by Mr Monet.

Katie looked at one called *A Field With Poppies*.
Wasn't that Jean, the painter's son, walking
through the field? Katie climbed in to see.

It was Jean! He was delighted to see her.

"We're going on a picnic!" he said, and Jean's mother said that Katie could join them.

They walked together, through the poppy field, looking for somewhere to sit.

Jean helped Katie gather armfuls of poppies for Grandma.

Afterwards they sat in the shade of the tree, the perfect place for a picnic. Mrs Monet opened a bag. She had bread and cheese and strawberries.

But Jean heard a buzzing noise and looked up. A black cloud of bees was flying towards them.

"They're after my poppies!" shouted Katie, her mouth
full of strawberries.

Jean and his mother ran towards the poppy field. But Katie
ran to the picture frame and dived into the gallery.

The bees followed Katie who ran on and on until she reached a window. She flung it open and threw the poppies out. The bees flew after them. Katie panted until she got her breath back. She still didn't have any flowers for Grandma!

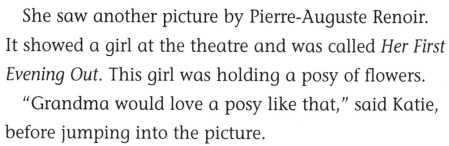

She saw another picture by Pierre-Auguste Renoir.
It showed a girl at the theatre and was called *Her First
Evening Out*. This girl was holding a posy of flowers.
  "Grandma would love a posy like that," said Katie,
before jumping into the picture.

"May I have your flowers?" asked
Katie. "I'll swap my hair ribbon."
"Hush," said the girl.
"The ballet is about to begin!"
Katie looked for a seat,
but they were all full. The
theatre manager appeared.
"*Mademoiselle*, may I see
your ticket?" he said.

Katie didn't have one so she ran off, down some steps.

She could hear the manager coming after her, so she opened a door to hide. On the other side people in colourful costumes shouted at Katie. So she ran away from them, towards some bright lights and the sound of music.

Katie pushed past heavy velvet curtains and found herself on stage. The dancers held their breath. So did the musicians in the orchestra. So did the audience. What was Katie going to do?

Katie danced! The music started up again and Katie pranced
all around the stage.

How the audience loved her! They had never seen anyone dance
so strangely before. They cheered and clapped and threw flowers.
Hundreds of flowers fell upon Katie as she twirled around.

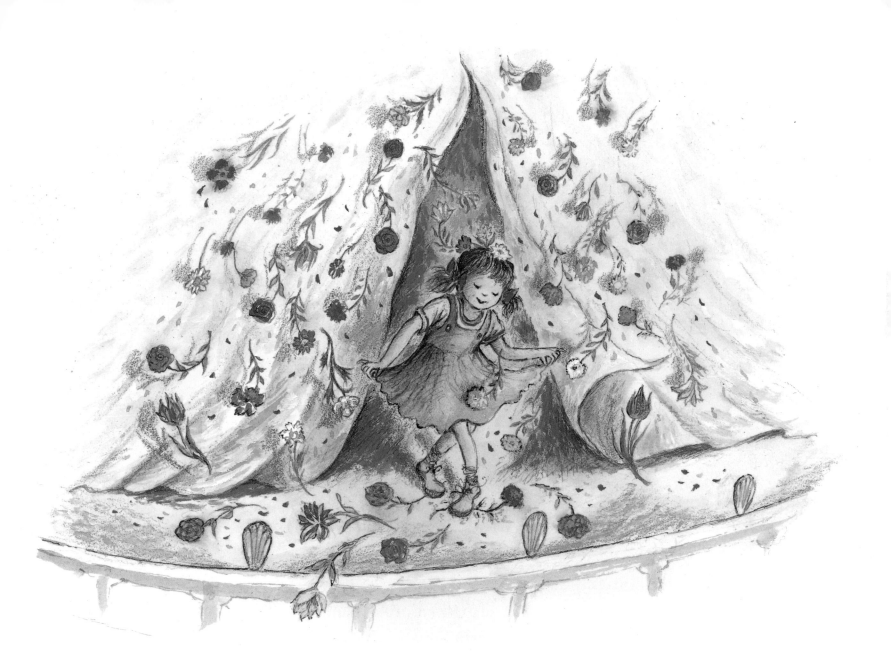

"Well done!" they shouted. "Bravo!"
When the music stopped, Katie curtsied and
gathered up her flowers.

The manager rushed over to her. "My dear, you have such talent!"

Katie blushed. "I just jumped around a bit really," she said.

"You must dance every night; you will be famous!" said the manager.

"Thanks, but it's Grandma's birthday," said Katie. "I must get back."

But Katie could not find her way to the picture frame. There were people everywhere changing costumes. She was afraid she might be stuck in the theatre picture forever!

All of a sudden she saw another frame.

"I must be in another picture!" said Katie. She gathered up her bouquet and climbed into the gallery.

Katie looked back at the picture. *The Blue Dancers* by Edgar Degas, she read. "I wonder if I would have been painted if I had stayed still long enough!" she said.

Then Katie ran over to her Grandma and gave her the flowers. "Happy Birthday, Grandma!"

"Oh, I say!" said Grandma. "Wherever did you get these
lovely flowers?"

Katie just laughed. But what was that in her pocket? It
was a paint brush! Mr Monet will need that, she thought.

She ran back to the first picture, left the brush on the
frame and then ran to catch up with her Grandma.

More about the Impressionists

The Impressionist painters lived in France at the end of the nineteenth century and the beginning of the twentieth century.

Their paintings tried to capture a precise moment in time (rather like a photograph) by recording an instant 'impression'. They painted their families, their gardens, trips to the theatre and all sorts of things they saw around them, often painting outside in the open air.

Their paintings, made up of blobs, were thought to be very modern and ugly to start with. Eventually people grew to love their 'impressions' because they were full of colour and movement, just like things in real life.

Claude Monet (1840-1926)

Monet loved to paint his family, gardens and landscapes. He painted *The Luncheon* and *The Field With Poppies* which are both at the Musée d'Orsay in Paris, France.

Pierre-Auguste Renoir (1841-1919)

Renoir was famous for painting portraits, especially of children and beautiful women. *The Girl With a Watering Can* can be seen in the National Gallery of Art in Washington DC, USA, and *Her First Evening Out* is in the National Gallery, London.

Edgar Degas (1834-1917)

Degas painted ballerinas and orchestras and theatres. He even made statues of ballet dancers. *The Blue Dancers* is now in the Musée d'Orsay in Paris, France.

There are other impressionist paintings by these and other great artists in museums and galleries all over the world.

Acknowledgements

The Luncheon by *Claude Monet*; Musée d'Orsay; © Photo RMN - H.Lewandowski (p5)

A Girl With a Watering Can by *Pierre-Auguste Renoir*; Chester Dale Collection; © Board of Trustees, National Gallery of Art, Washington DC (p10)

The Field With Poppies by *Claude Monet*; Musée d'Orsay; © Photo RMN - H.Lewandowski (p15)

Her First Evening Out by *Pierre-Auguste Renoir*; Reproduced by courtesy of the Trustees of the National Gallery, London (p21)

The Blue Dancers by *Edgar Degas*; Musée d'Orsay; © Photo RMN - Préveral (p30)